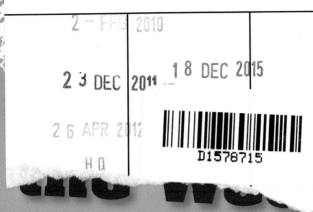

Sam
Carter

Illustrated by
Dan Chernett

To Richard Lount and Dean Fullalove - my own
(totally cool) geeks of the week! ;-) DS

First published in 2009
by Franklin Watts

Text © Deborah Smith 2009
Illustrations © Dan Chernett 2009
Cover design by Peter Scoulding

Franklin Watts
338 Euston Road
London NW1 3BH

Franklin Watts Australia
Level 17/207 Kent Street
Sydney, NSW 2000

ISBN: 978 0 7496 9041 0

1 3 5 7 9 10 8 6 4 2

Printed in Great Britain

Franklin Watts is a division of Hachette Children's Books,
an Hachette UK company.
www.hachette.co.uk

Harvey, Sam, Amber, Ravi, Jade and Lewis are:

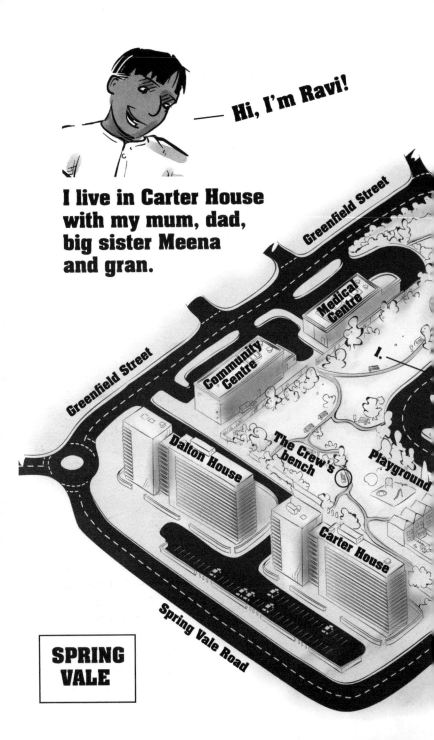

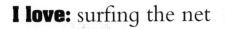

I love: surfing the net

I hate: bullies

I want to be: a computer game maker

Best word: *Google*

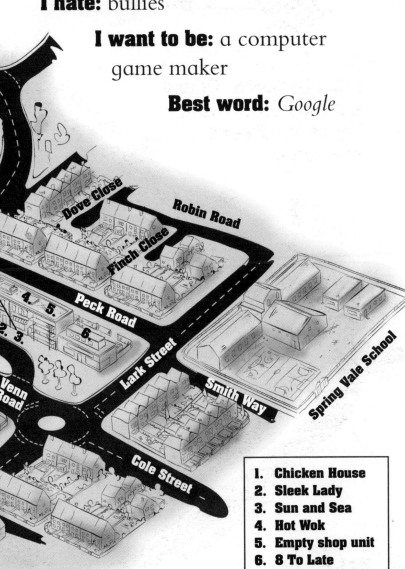

Dove Close

Robin Road

Finch Close

Peck Road

Lark Street

Smith Way

Spring Vale School

Venn Road

Cole Street

1. **Chicken House**
2. **Sleek Lady**
3. **Sun and Sea**
4. **Hot Wok**
5. **Empty shop unit**
6. **8 To Late**

Chapter One

"Good news!" my mum says one morning.

I look up from my cereal and computer mag.

"Jay is coming to visit," she tells us.

"Cousin Jay, from New York?" I ask.

Mum nods. "He will be here for a week," she says. "He can share your room."

New York! Wait till I tell the Crew!

7

"So what's Jay like?" Amber asks.

"Dunno – I've never met him," I say.

Harvey shrugs. "Hey, he's a New Yorker – he's gotta be cool!"

"Not like Ravi then," says Lewis.

Jade gives him a shove.

But it's true – I'm not cool.

Harvey says I'm a geek.

Coz I love computers and stuff.

But being a geek can come in handy.

Like when I help the Crew with maths homework.

Then Harvey calls me the Geek of the Week!

I can't wait for Jay to arrive now.

A week with a cool cousin…

…maybe he'll help me to be cool!

Chapter Two

We go to meet Jay at the airport.

I've made a big sign with Jay's full name on it.

"He won't miss that!" Dad says with a grin.

And then we hear a shout.

"Hi! Here I am!"

This must be Jay, running up to us.

I stare at him.

And so do loads of other people!

He has on a really loud shirt…

Baggy shorts…

Long white socks – with sandals…

He dresses like my dad!

New York cool?

Er… I don't THINK so!

"Hey, guys!" Jay yells.

He holds his arms open wide.

Oh no – he wants us to HUG?

Not cool.

"Ravi!" Jay yells. "So great to meet you!"

"Er…yeah, you too," I mutter into his jacket.

Boy, is he big!

And loud!

Chapter Three

When we get home I help Jay to unpack.

Out come more loud shirts.

More baggy shorts.

More long white socks.

Oh my days… An 'IT CLUB' T-shirt!

Jay isn't a bit of a geek, like me.

No. He is a TOTAL geek.

But then I see his games console.

"Wow!" I say. "That's the best one, innit!"

OK. So that's pretty cool.

It's time to meet the Crew.

"I can't wait to meet them," Jay tells me.

But what will they think of him?

We walk over to the bench.

The rest of the Crew are kicking a ball around.

They stop playing when they see us.

Lewis looks down at Jay's sandals and socks.

His mouth falls open.

"Hey – you must be Jay," Amber calls.

Jay nods. "Good to meet you all," he says.

Harvey jogs over, grinning. "You too, man," he says.

Then he points to Jay's sandals. "Nice shoes!"

Harvey is a joker.

"Thanks!" says Jay. "And I like your pants!"

Harvey steps back, shocked.

"My what?" he says.

Jay points to Harvey's combat trousers.

"Your pants," he says again.

"Jay, in England those are trousers, not pants!" Amber tells him.

Lewis shows Jay the top of his pants.

"These are pants!" he says.

Jay grins. "In America, those are shorts!" he says.

Lewis scratches his head.

Boy, this week is gonna be tricky!

Chapter Four

The Dalton House Crew come over.

"Match time!" says Sam.

I turn to Jay. "Do you wanna play football?" I ask him.

"Nooooo!" he says. "I have two left feet!"

"You can't be as bad as Lewis!" jokes Harvey.

Lewis grins and gives him a shove.

So Jay shrugs and says, "OK, count me in."

Denzil kicks off with a pass to Marcus.

Harvey tackles – and gets control of the ball.

He passes to Amber – but kicks it wide.

It shoots past her and lands at Jay's feet.

"Go, Jay!" we yell.

He starts to run down the field with the ball.

Then he trips over, coz of his geeky sandals!

"Woah! Sorry, guys!" he calls.

Marcus gets the ball again.

He shoots it past Lewis – and into the goal.

"Sweet one, bro!" Denzil yells.

We're 1–0 down.

Then Amber scores.

1–1 – our turn to cheer.

Harvey takes the ball to the middle.

But just then, his mum comes over.

She has Harvey's little sister with her.

"Tia's nursery is closed today," she tells him.

"She will have to stay home with you."

Then she rushes off to work.

Harvey drops the ball.

"Better count me out, guys!" he says with a frown.

"Hey, I'll watch Tia," Jay offers. "You can play."

Harvey beams at him. "Thanks, bro!" he says.

Jay and Tia go and sit on the bench.

But then it starts to rain.

Jay gives Tia his cap and coat.

"Next goal wins?" Denzil asks.

We all agree – and keep on playing.

Then Tia yells, "Harveeeey!"

Harvey stops running with the ball.

"What?" he yells back.

"I'm getting wet!" Tia tells him.
"I wanna go home!"

Next thing, Denzil hooks the ball away from Harvey.

He bombs down the field – and scores.

Nooo!

We lose.

"Gotta keep your eye on the ball, bro!" Denzil calls.

He and his crew run off back to Dalton House.

We all shrug, like we don't care.

"Win some, lose some," I say.

Then we hurry to Harvey's place, out of the rain.

Chapter Five

"Hey! You got *Burn Up*!" Jay says.

He picks up the box. "Now we're talking!"

His face is one big grin.

"So what's your score?" Sam asks him.

"691," Jay tells us.

We all stare.

"Respect!" I say. "My best is 328."

"And Ravi is the *Burn Up* man!" says Lewis.

Harvey brings out some eats.

Then we load *Burn Up* on the TV.

"Let's use crash mode," Harvey says.

"Great – it's the best!" agrees Jay.

Harvey and Jay go first.

Jay is soon in the lead.

His pile-ups are massive!

And so is his score!

"Wow! How do you do that?"
Lewis asks.

Jay grins. "I'll show you some tricks,"
he says.

Jay starts a new game.

"Turn at this corner," he tells us.

"Coz there are more cars to crash – see?"

BANG! A MASSIVE crash!

Jay's points zoom up.

"And turn here!" he says.

BANG! Again!

"My turn now!" I say. I can't wait!

I take the wheel from Harvey and sit next to Jay.

I use his tricks – and my score goes up to 465!

Tia stands in front of the TV.

"Tia! Move out of the way!" we all yell.

She stamps her foot and sticks out her lip.

"I'm bored!" she says.

Harvey rolls his eyes.

"Do you wanna play Magic House?" he asks her.

"Yeah!" she says.

Harvey goes over to the computer.

He opens up Magic House, a game for little kids.

"Why don't we go online too?"
Jay asks.

"We can play the new *Burn Up
Street Race*."

"Ooh, that sounds cool!" Amber says.

We all agree, and log on.

Then Jay puts in his player name –
JayPlay1998.

We stare at him.

"YOU are JayPlay1998?" I say.

Jay nods.

"We've seen you on the games sites!"
Jade tells him.

"Yeah, you win loads!" says Sam.

"Wow! My cuz is JayPlay1998, innit!" I yell.

Jay goes a bit red.

"Well, Nik in my IT Club wins more than me," he says.

But he looks well pleased.

"Look!" says Harvey. "We got a message!"

It's from the Dalton House Crew.

They are playing *Football Pro*.

HELLO LOSERS. WANNA LOSE AGAIN?

WE'LL GIVE YA A GAME.

"No way!" Amber says. "They always beat us online."

"Even with Ravi," Sam adds.

"But what about with JayPlay1998?" I ask.

I look at Jay.

He grins and nods. "*Burn-Up Street Race* can wait," he says.

Then he sends a message back.

BRING IT ON!

Chapter Six

Jay leads the game.

Me, Harvey and Sam play with him.

The others watch and cheer.

Jay is no good at football in the real world. But online he rocks!

"Go, Jay! Go, Jay!" we yell.

We thrash Dalton House – three times!

Then they log off. Sweet!

"That was just the best, innit!" I say.

"Harveeey!" Tia calls. "Magic House has gone all funny!"

"Hang on, Tia!" Harvey calls back.

"But Harveeey!" she calls again. "It's melting!"

Jay leaps up from the sofa.

"Uh-oh… Sounds like Melt Down!"
he says.

He runs over to the computer.

We all follow.

"What's Melt Down?" Harvey asks.

"It's a computer virus," I tell him.

Harvey looks well stressed now.

"But all Mum's college work is on there!" he yells. "We have to save it!"

We all look at Jay.

He sits down at the computer.

"I'll do my best," he says.

He starts to tap loads of keys.

Weird screens come up.

We all watch and wait.

And then, at last, he says, "Done!"

Harvey slaps Jay on the back.

"Thanks, bro!" he says. "You're a lifesaver!"

Then he touches fists with me.

"Geeky can be good, man!" he says.

"Yeah," I agree. And I touch fists with Jay.

"Your turn to be Geek of the Week, cuz! Innit!"

Good Luck, Bad Luck

It's Saturday morning.

Mum is out at the shops.

Dad has gone to work at Hot Wok.

I can stay in bed as long as I want.

Later, I can hang out with the Crew.

Saturdays are the best!

I turn over, for just one more snooze…

I'm up now and WIDE AWAKE.

I've got loads of time until I meet the Crew.

I wash, get dressed and have some toast and jam.

Then I go and check my e-mail.

What's this one?

OPEN ME NOW – TO STOP BAD LUCK!

Will this be Jade's lucky day?

Jade checks her e-mail — and finds a nasty chain letter. It says that she and the Crew will have bad luck all day! OH, NO! Jade must save them!

Catch up with all

   the **CREW** adventures!

978 0 7496 9038 0

978 0 7496 9039 7

978 0 7496 9042 7

978 0 7496 9041 0

978 0 7496 9040 3

978 0 7496 9037 3